Fisherwoman

Effie Adrienne

MACMILLAN

Macmillan Education
Between Towns Road, Oxford OX4 3PP
A division of Macmillan Publishers Limited
Companies and representatives throughout the world

www.macmillan-caribbean.com

ISBN 978 0 333 74143 6

First published 1999

Printed in Malaysia

2010 2009 2008
18 17 16 15 14 13 12 11 10

Sammy lived by the sea with his father and mother. His father, Franklin, was a fisherman.

One day, during the school holidays, Sammy's father called to him, 'Sammy! Where are you? Come here and clean the boat engine! Sammy, where are you?' He sounded angry.

Sammy was in the kitchen. The window was shut, so he did not hear his father. He was peeling a pumpkin. It was fat and yellow.

'I like being in the kitchen,' thought Sammy. 'I like the smell of spices and vegetables. I like cooking.'

Outside, Sammy's father shouted again, louder this time, 'Sammy! Are you in the kitchen again? Come out now! The kitchen isn't a place for boys!'

Sammy's father often said, 'Cooking is only for girls.' So he got angry whenever Sammy spent time in the kitchen.

'Sammy! Sammy!' he yelled. This time Sammy heard him, even though the window was shut.

Sammy stopped peeling the pumpkin. He opened the window and said, 'I'm coming, Father. Let me finish this first.' He picked up the pumpkin again. 'I'd rather cook than clean the boat engine,' he thought.

But suddenly the kitchen door flew open. Sammy's father stood in the doorway.

'Sammy, I'm very cross with you,' he said.

'Please, Father,' said Sammy, 'let me do this. Mother's at the shop. I want to help her.'

'You want to help?' said his father. 'Go and clean the boat engine, then. That's a job for a boy. I've told you a hundred times, the kitchen isn't a place for boys.'

Sammy said, 'But Father, Mr Harris says ...'

'Who's Mr Harris?' his father said sharply.

'Mr Harris is our new teacher,' said Sammy. 'He says, "Boys and girls are equal and they can do the same things. They can both choose what to do." So girls can clean boat engines and boys can cook, if they want to.'

'Why is your teacher teaching you these things?' complained his father. 'You go to school to learn reading and writing. You don't go to school to learn to be a girl.'

Sammy said softly, 'But Father, don't you understand? I'm not learning to be a girl. I just want you to let me do the things I like. Why can't I help Mother? Mr Harris says …'

His father yelled, 'I don't care what Mr Harris says! I'm your father. You'll do as I say. Now go out and clean the boat engine.'

'Can I finish this first?' asked Sammy, 'and clean the engine afterwards?'

'No, you can't!' his father roared. 'Get out there now! Get out or I'll beat you!'

Sammy felt like crying. He thought, 'Why do I always have to do what Father wants? It's not fair.'

As he cleaned the boat engine, Sammy thought, 'Why
doesn't Father listen to me? I'm not a child any more, I'm
twelve years old. Why can't he understand that I'd rather
cook than clean this?' He rubbed hard with an oily rag.

Soon Sammy's mother came back home and went to the kitchen to cook. She saw the pumpkin and smiled.

She opened the window. 'Good, Sammy, you've done the pumpkin,' she said. 'Now I'll cook the meat.'

Sammy wanted to help her but the boat engine was still not clean enough.

His father came out. He looked more kindly at his son now. 'You're doing a good job, Sammy,' he said. 'It's a very important job. We must keep the engine clean because a dirty engine is dangerous. You have to look after boats.'

Then he went to the veranda. He always sat on the veranda when Mother was cooking.

When Sammy went inside for dinner, it started to rain. His mother looked up and said, 'I think it's going to rain all night.'

As they ate, she said, 'There's very little meat left. Soon we'll have no food left in the house. And we haven't any money to buy more.'

'Don't worry,' said Sammy's father. 'Tomorrow I'll go fishing. We can have fish. And breadfruits too. There are some nice big breadfruits in the tree, just right for picking. In the morning I'll climb the tree and get some.'

'But it's going to rain all night,' said Sammy's mother. 'The branches will be wet and slippery in the morning. You'll slip and fall from the tree. Please wait for it to dry.'

'Nonsense, Cora,' said his father. 'I'll climb the tree and I'll be fine.'

Sammy ate his food quietly. He thought, 'Father never listens to anyone.'

It rained all night. The next morning, Sammy went outside.

His mother was calling to his father. 'You mustn't climb the tree, Franklin,' she was saying. 'It's wet from the rain. You'll slip and fall.'

Sammy's father just laughed. He started to climb the tree. The branches shook and water fell from the leaves.

When he got to the
top of the tree, he broke
off a breadfruit and threw
it down.

Sammy's mother
caught it. 'One is enough,'
she said. 'It's a nice big
one. Come down now.'

'There are plenty more,' said his father.

Sammy looked up. There were lots of breadfruits with big glistening raindrops all over them.

'Franklin, please come down now,' urged his mother.

'No, I'll just break off one more,' said his father. And he reached for another breadfruit.

But just at that moment his foot slipped on a wet branch and he came crashing down.

'My leg!' he cried. 'I can't get up!'

His wife and son ran to help him.

'Oh! I think he's broken his leg,' cried Sammy's mother. 'Sammy, run to the store! Quickly! Ask Mrs Daley to call an ambulance. Run, Sammy, run!'

At the hospital, the doctor said, 'Yes, Mr Johnson, your leg is broken. It will take time to heal. You can't go fishing until the plaster comes off. That will be four or five weeks.'

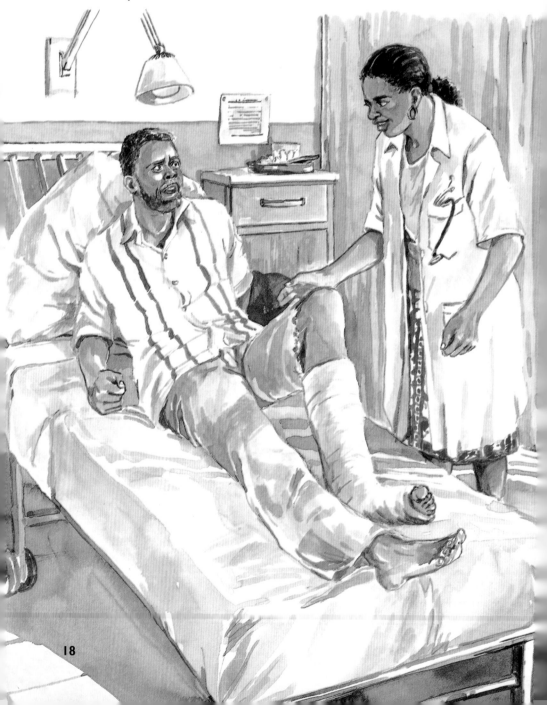

It was late when Sammy's father returned home.

'Help me, Sammy,' he said. 'I've never used crutches before.'

'Don't worry, Father,' said Sammy. 'I'll help you.' He felt sorry for him.

'Come and eat, Franklin,' said Sammy's mother. 'Now I've boiled some breadfruit just the way you like it best. Nice and soft, with a little butter.'

Sammy's father was worried. 'I need to go fishing,' he said. 'If I don't get some fish, what else can we eat?'

'We have a few tomatoes left,' said his wife. 'And some plantain. That's all.'

'But now I can't go fishing,' said Sammy's father. 'What are we going to do? We've no money to buy food.'

Even as he ate the breadfruit, Sammy began to feel hungry. 'There won't be much for us to eat tomorrow!' he thought.

'Don't worry,' said his mother. 'I'll go fishing tomorrow.'

Sammy looked up.

'Fishing, woman?' shouted Sammy's father. 'You can't do that!'

'Why not?' asked his mother.

'Because you're a woman,' said his father. 'Fishing isn't a job for a woman. It's a job for a man.'

'Nonsense,' said Sammy's mother. 'We're poor. We need fish to eat and we need fish to sell, to get money. Fish is fish. It doesn't matter who goes fishing.'

'No, we'll find another way,' said his father. 'You can't go fishing and that's that. You won't find any fish and you'll get lost at sea.'

Sammy's mother laughed. 'I won't get lost,' she said. 'I'll find plenty of fish and I'll find my way back home. My father was a fisherman. He taught me how to fish and I haven't forgotten.'

'But you can't sail my boat,' said Sammy's father.

'Yes, I can,' answered his mother. 'It's just like my father's boat. Look, this is how you start it …'

She undid her apron and pulled at the string. 'The cord goes to the engine. You pull it and the engine fires.'

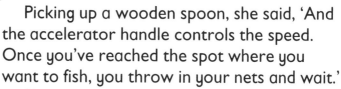

Picking up a wooden spoon, she said, 'And the accelerator handle controls the speed. Once you've reached the spot where you want to fish, you throw in your nets and wait.'

She crossed her arms and looked at her husband.

'I'm tired of arguing,' said Sammy's father. 'I can't stop you. But I know it will end badly.'

The next morning Sammy helped his mother to get the boat out. 'Let me come with you, Mother,' he said. 'I can help you to fish.'

'No, Sammy,' said his mother. 'You stay here with your father. With his broken leg, he needs help. Also, you can keep him from worrying about me. I'll be home before sunset.'

Some people came to watch. 'Look, a woman's going fishing!' they cried.

The boat left the shore, then it became smaller and smaller. The sea looked huge and scary. Sammy felt worried. Then the boat disappeared completely.

Sammy went inside. His father was sitting by the window. 'Don't worry, Father,' Sammy said. 'Mother will be back before sunset.' But, secretly, he too was very worried.

Sammy and his father sat quietly, looking out to sea. Time passed slowly. A wind rose and the sea grew rough.

Sammy's father said, 'I'm worried about your mother. She doesn't know how to fish. She'll get lost.'

'No,' said Sammy. 'Mother'll be fine. Her father was a fisherman and he taught her how to fish.'

But really he was getting more and more worried. The afternoon seemed very long.

He thought, 'Mother'll be back before sunset.'

But his mother was still not home when the sun started to set. The sky grew black and orange. The breadfruit tree stood out, dark against the stormy sky.

Sammy thought, 'Will I ever see Mother again?' He felt sick in his stomach.

He went down to the beach. The wind was bending the palm trees over. A small crowd was standing and looking out to sea.

The sea was growing darker. There was no sign of a boat.

'Mother, where are you? Please come back,' Sammy prayed. He wanted to cry.

Then a shape appeared on the water, but at first Sammy could not see what it was.

Slowly, the shape grew clearer.
'It's a boat!' Hope filled Sammy's heart.
But no! The shape was just a shadow on the water.
Sammy's heart sank.

But wait, there was another, smaller shape. It was coming closer! The shape was his father's boat!

'Father, Father!' yelled Sammy. 'Mother's back!'

His father hobbled down the steps on his crutches.

Everyone on the beach helped to pull the boat in.

Sammy's mother looked tired but happy. 'There were so many fish to catch!' she said.

Sammy hugged her.

His father looked in the boat. 'That's a huge catch!' he said. The fish shone like silver in the boat.

At last Sammy's father looked up. 'Cora, I'm proud of you,' he said. 'You really do know how to fish!'

Now all the people started shouting, 'Fisherwoman! Fisherwoman! The first fisherwoman in our village!'

A man said, 'Fisherwoman, how much is your fish?'
Everyone gathered round to buy the fish.

Sammy's father put some fish to one side. 'These are for us,' he said. And he held up the biggest, fattest fish of all. 'Tonight we'll celebrate Cora's big catch.'

The people bought all the other fish. Sammy put the money in a small bag.

Sammy and his father and mother went home.

'Now I must cook the fish,' said his mother.

'No,' said his father. 'Let me cook it. You're tired.'

'But your leg's broken,' said his mother. 'You need to rest.'

Sammy's father said, 'My leg's broken and I can't go fishing. But I can cook. I don't need a leg for cooking! You need to rest, not me. Go and sit on the veranda.'

In the kitchen, Sammy said, 'Father, I'll prepare the spices.'

'And I'll clean the fish,' said his father. Sammy put a chair for him by the sink.

After a while, Sammy said, 'Let's season the fish.' He started to rub spices into the fish. Then he stopped. 'But Father, you haven't taken the scales off the fish!' he said. It was so funny. But Sammy was afraid to laugh.

Suddenly Sammy's father laughed. He laughed and laughed and laughed. 'Look at me,' he said. 'I'm a fisherman and I can't even clean a fish. Isn't that silly?'

Now Sammy laughed too. He said, 'Don't worry, Father. I'll show you. We'll clean the fish together.'

Together, Sammy and his father scraped the scales off
the fish. The scales flew everywhere. They flew into Sammy's
hair, but he did not care. He was happy now.

'Father's not shouting,' he thought. 'He's talking. He's
listening. And he's cooking!'

His father said, 'Sammy, when I was a boy, I never
cooked. My mother said, "Cooking's for girls". That's why
I can't cook. But now I'm going to learn.'

'And I'll help you,' said Sammy.

Sammy's mother came in. 'I heard laughter,' she said.

'Yes, Cora,' said Sammy's father. 'Sammy and I are cooking together, and we're laughing together. Come and join us.'

CARIBBEAN HOP STEP JUMPS

Series Listing

HOP

Click Flash   Barbara Applin   0-333-92077-5
Ping Pong Pan   Barbara Applin   0-333-74142-0
The School that Sank   Sherry North   0-333-97658-4
Water for Monique   Shelley Davidow & Catherine Parrill   0-333-97429-8

STEP

The Angry Mountain   Claudette Megan Adams   0-333-74144-7
Carly and the Crabholes   Natalie Williams   0-333-95445-9
Gary the Smartest Gecko   Thalia Bell   0-333-95446-7
Gyp's Puppies   Sandra Browne   1-4050-2514-X
Ninety-nine Potcakes   Alice Bain   0-333-97659-2
Saving Mr Omardeen   Judy Stone   0-333-77623-2
The Scottish Island Girl   Joanne Johnson   0-333-92091-0
Shauna's Hurricane   Francine Jacobs   1-4050-1701-5

JUMP

Digger's Diner   Joanne Johnson   1-4050-2467-4
Fire and Steel   Judy Stone   0-333-77622-4
Fisherwoman   Effie Adrienne   0-333-74143-9
Go! Krabita! Go!   Petronella Breinburg   0-333-95305-3
Jeremia and the Trumpet Man   Petronella Breinburg   0-333-92065-1
Running for Real   Marcia Francois   0-333-92234-4
Sally's Way   Joanne Johnson   0-333-95450-5
The Taming of Pudding-Pan   Berna McIntosh   0-333-74141-2
The Village Storyteller   Claudette Megan Adams   0-333-97632-0